dream
BOATS

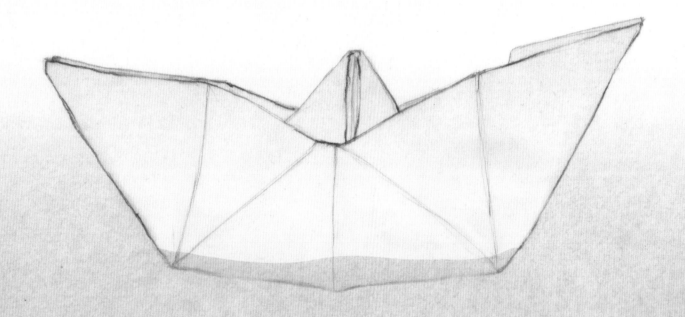

SIMPLY READ BOOKS

dream BOATS

story DAN BAR-EL

illustrations KIRSTI ANNE WAKELIN

I don't have naps. I have adventures.
I don't sleep in a bed. I ride in a Dream Boat.

You have your very own Dream Boat too.
Close your eyes.
Untie the moorings.
Then push off from shore.

Water is memory; water is dreams.
Clear or mirror, deep as sleep,
        water flows inward and Dream Boats follow.
Take me, Dream Boat, and show me everything I know.

*M*aiqui rows across cold waters. High in the Andes Mountains, it is night. But it is not dark. Mighty Viracocha, maker of light, reaches into the shimmering lake. He tosses up stars that paint the sky with constellations. One is Yacana, the thirsty llama.

And then a real llama greets Maiqui at the shore. *Hello, friend.*
Together they journey down treeless slopes past terraces of barley
and quinoa towards his grandparents' village. Maiqui hears music
and sees dancing. He dances too, tickled by flute song.

*A*ljuu's cedar canoe floats towards the shores
of Haida Gwaii. Eagle, Orca and Black Bear stare
out at her from the mist. They stand silent and still.
Come, child. Grandmother's soft voice leads Aljuu
through rainforest, along carpets of moss. Now
they are on Rose Spit, picking wild strawberries.
High above, Raven's laugh fills the air.

Sun turns to fire. Aljuu watches her brothers and cousins drum together during the potlatch. She feels the *thump, thump* beat all through her body.

Water softens. It separates.
It yawns in the sunlight like dewdrops, like glass.
But Dream Boats bind water like fingers, like eyelashes.

Dream Boats weave streams into oceans
    and stories into blankets.

Dream Boats braid magic with Mondays
    and wishes with tears.

Dream Boats carry the oldest maps.

Parvati sits among nets laden with fish as she rides towards Mumbai. Her boat is old and creaky. *But what's that? Rain falling from a blue sky?* No, it's not rain. Giant Ganesh lifts his long trunk and sprays an arc of diamonds. He waves his four hands as Parvati passes under. Parvati waves back, her happy face among an ocean of smiles on a warm August day.

On Chowpatty Beach, she perches on
her father's shoulders and touches clouds.

*I*van sails into St. Petersburg upon a mighty Russian frigate. The heavy oak ship groans with each crashing wave. Topsails boom with each wind gust. But Ivan is not afraid. He stands steady above the lion-headed bow. *Look, there! Up ahead! Bear Spirits!*

Night tumbles fast beneath galloping hooves.
Ivan sneaks beneath the bony legs of Baba Yaga.
Aha! Found it! He picks up a feather shed by the
Firebird. Beautiful, dazzling rainbow feather. Ivan
offers it to his mother and together they sip tea.

Your dreams and my dreams, my dreams and yours,
Dream Boats entwine on oceans of memory.
We wave. We touch hands. We promise to meet soon.

Babatúndé plants a long pole into the swampy waters of the Niger River. He pushes against it hard. The small boat glides past mangrove trees with tangles of thick roots reaching higher than houses. And then... *Grandfather!*

Into the sacred forest where trees reveal masks and drums jabber stories. *Behold, Babatúndé.* From the sky, Obatala, the boy-god, descends on a spider's thread. From a snail shell he tosses dirt until the ground turns dry and solid. Chameleon approves, then vanishes within a blush of color. Babatúndé leaves too, lured by the scent of spicy stew. Auntie pounds yams while Grandmother folds fufu for him to scoop and swallow.

Jiang-Li sits high at the stern of her trustworthy junk. Silently, she snakes through the curves of the Yangtze River. The smooth slatted sails open like giant fans, now golden in the setting sun. On the banks she sees lotus flowers. And then she spies old Chang Kuo-lao riding backwards on his magic donkey. *Hey, wait for me!* Jiang-Li rides with him through a forest of poems and paper lanterns.

Clang! A gong smashes in the dark. It is New Year's Eve.
Jiang-Li holds her mother's hand and together they cross
over three bridges. *Ka-rak-crack-crack-crack!* Firecrackers
echo in the busy streets. *Ka-rak-crack-crack-crack!*
Jiang-Li hugs her father's leg tight.

Water is memory; water is dreams.
Sometimes storm clouds gather.
Sometimes it rains and it rains.
Dream Boats rock. Dream Boats sway.
But Dream Boats find safe harbour.

Tide flows in. Water touches land.
It leaves its print, then hides.
Dream Boats return too.
They dock gently, then fade.

Eyes open. Bodies stretch. Friends call out our names.

It's time to play. Time to tell tales of adventure.

Do you remember?

Do you want to go back?

Would you remember the way?

Not to worry. Dream Boats remember.

Call them and they will come.

for Beatrice
DAN

for all the dreamers, young and grown
KIRSTI

*D*an Bar-el is an award-winning children's author, educator and storyteller. His writing includes chapter books, picture books and a recent graphic novel. His picture book *Pussycat, Pussycat, Where Have You Been?*, illustrated by Rae Mate and published by Simply Read Books, was a finalist for both the 2012 Marilyn Baillie Picture Book Award and the 2012 Christie Harris Illustrated Children's Literature Prize. Dan currently travels across the country visiting schools and libraries presenting his books, giving storytelling performances and leading a variety of writing workshops. He shares his life with artist and goldsmith Dominique Bréchault. *danbar-el.com*

*K*irsti Anne Wakelin is an illustrator and designer who lives, works and daydreams in Vancouver, B.C. She has illustrated several picture books for children including *Looking for Loons*, published by Simply Read Books. *mysecretelephant.com*

Glossary

There are many myths and folktales referenced in this book. As there are numerous sources to draw from, all with subtle and not-so-subtle variations, choices inevitably had to be made, and sometimes amalgamations were created. Below are some brief explanations of the myths and folktales mentioned.

Baba Yaga An old witch who is considered to be evil, yet also a source of guidance. There are many tales about Baba Yaga. In some, she is said to have three riders, one of whom is Night, dressed in black and riding a black horse.

Bear Spirits Many old cultures in northern lands such as Russia both worshipped and feared Bear Spirits.

Chang Kuo-lao One of the eight immortals of Taoism. He was an old hermit with a magical donkey that he rode backwards. The donkey could travel great distances in a single day and then turn into paper, which Chang Kuo-lao would fold up and put in his pocket.

Crossing Three Bridges An old Shanghai tradition, during the celebration of the lunar New Year, has mothers and children crossing three bridges to dispel diseases.

The Firebird From a Slavic fairytale that contains a magical, glowing bird. In one version, young Prince Ivan discovers the bird stealing golden apples from his father's orchard. He tries to catch it but only manages to pull out a single feather.

Ganesh A Hindu deity that is depicted with the head of an elephant and many arms. Ganesh is known as the god of wisdom and prosperity.

Obatala and the Chameleon There are different versions of the Yoruba creation myth. Obatala is the son of Olorun, the supreme creator god. With the world being nothing but water and air, he is sent down by his father to make the world solid using sand and a chicken that pecks at it and spreads it about. In one version, Olorun sends a chameleon to check on Obatala's work.

Raven There are many legends attributed to Raven, the trickster-creator, but one Haida story tells of how Raven helped the first humans emerge from a giant clam shell that beached upon Rose Spit.

Viracocha A powerful Inca god believed to have created the sun, moon and stars.

Yacana One of the constellations that Viracocha created was the llama Yacana, who would drink up the waters of the ocean and in doing so, would prevent future floods.

PUBLISHED IN 2013 BY SIMPLY READ BOOKS

www.simplyreadbooks.com

Text © 2013 Dan Bar-el   Illustrations © 2013 Kirsti Anne Wakelin

LIBRARY AND ARCHIVES CANADA CATALOGUING IN PUBLICATION

Bar-el, Dan   Dream boats / written by Dan Bar-el ; illustrated by Kirsti Anne Wakelin.   ISBN 978-1-897476-87-1
Wakelin, Kirsti Anne II. Title.   PS8553.A76229D74 2012   jC813'.54   C2011-906854-0

MANUFACTURED IN MALAYSIA   10 9 8 7 6 5 4 3 2 1

*We gratefully acknowledge for their financial support of our publishing program the Canada Council for the Arts,
the BC Arts Council, and the Government of Canada through the Canada Book Fund (CBF).*

*The artwork for this book was created in a wide range of traditional media, including ink, watercolour, acrylic,
willow charcoal and pencil on vellum and paper, in combination with ephemera and textiles, and finished digitally.*
BOOK DESIGN BY KIRSTI WAKELIN. TEXT SET IN ASHBURY REGULAR AND ITALIC, CALLUNA SANS REGULAR, AND RABIOHEAD.